SLIP STREAM

UNARMED AND DANGEROUS

DAVID AND **HELEN ORME**
Illustrated by **DAN CHERNETT**

TITLES AT THIS LEVEL

Fiction

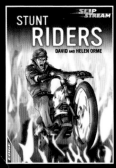

978 1 4451 1314 2 pb

978 1 4451 1316 6 pb

978 1 4451 1318 0 pb

Graphic fiction

978 1 4451 1322 7 pb

978 1 4451 1320 3 pb

978 1 4451 1324 1 pb

Non-fiction

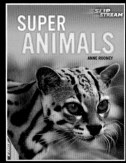

978 1 4451 1308 1

978 1 4451 1310 4

978 1 4451 1312 8

UNARMED AND DANGEROUS

DAVID AND HELEN ORME
Illustrated by DAN CHERNETT

EDGE
FRANKLIN WATTS

LONDON·SYDNEY

First published in 2012 by
Franklin Watts
338 Euston Road
London NW1 3BH

Franklin Watts Australia
Level 17/207 Kent Street
Sydney NSW 2000

Text © David and Helen Orme 2012
Illustration © Franklin Watts 2012

The rights of David and Helen Orme to be
identified as the authors and Dan Chernett
as the illustrator of this Work have been
asserted in accordance with the Copyright,
Designs and Patents Act, 1988.

A CIP catalogue record for this book is
available from the British Library.

ISBN 978 1 4451 1316 6

Series Editors: Adrian Cole and Jackie Hamley
Series Advisors: Diana Bentley and Dee Reid
Series Designer: Peter Scoulding

1 3 5 7 9 10 8 6 4 2

Printed in China

Franklin Watts is a division of
Hachette Children's Books,
an Hachette UK company.
www.hachette.co.uk

CONTENTS

CHAPTER 1
HELP NEEDED

"Your Mum is ill today. I need your help in the shop," said Dad.

Nita was cross. It was a nice day.
She wanted to be outside.

"You can start by filling up the shelves,"

said Dad.

But Nita had a plan.

If she was rubbish at helping in the shop,

Dad would soon get fed up.

CHAPTER 2
EGG PILE UP

First Dad asked Nita to stack some eggs.

Nita had an idea. She could have fun stacking the eggs.

A customer came in.

He took a box of eggs from the top of the pile.

The pile wobbled then crashed to the floor.

The mess went all over his shoes.

"Argh! Look at my shoes!" he said crossly.

Then he walked out of the shop.

CHAPTER 3
CLEAN UP JOB

Nita's dad was cross.

"Can't you even get a simple job right?" he asked.

"Sorry," said Nita. "I'd better get out of your way."

"Oh no you don't," said Dad. "Get this mess

cleaned up – now!"

Nita put some water in a bucket.

Then she got a mop.

"You must warn customers about

the wet floor," said Dad. "I don't want

them slipping and hurting themselves."

Nita was rubbish at mopping.

She splashed too much water on the floor.

CHAPTER 4
DAYLIGHT ROBBERY

Just then the shop door burst open.

Two men rushed in.

The first man was carrying a gun.

The second man had a knife.

"Open the till and give us the money!"

said the first man.

Then he slipped on the wet floor.

The second man crashed into him.

The knife stabbed the first man in the leg.

He dropped his gun.

The second man fell backwards.

He smashed his head on the shelves.

Nita picked up the gun.

"Dad, phone the police quick!" she shouted.

CHAPTER 5
OFF THE HOOK?

Dad said Nita had done really well.

"So can I go out now?" she asked.

"OK," said Dad. "But first, you've

got to clean up all this mess!"

STUNT
RIDERS

DAVID AND HELEN ORME

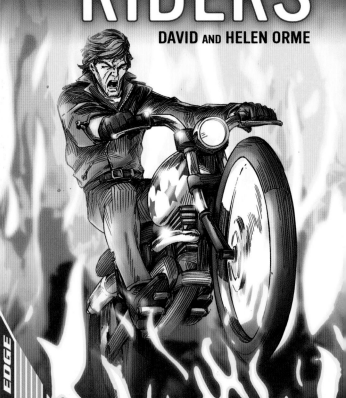

Zak and Jed are stunt bike riders. Dan comes
to see their show. He wants to be a stunt bike rider too.

Zak and Jed do the exploding coffin trick. Everyone cheers!
They are the best stunt riders in the world.
But what is their secret?

LONDON•SYDNEY

SLIP
STREAM

WALK INTO
DANGER

DAVID AND HELEN ORME

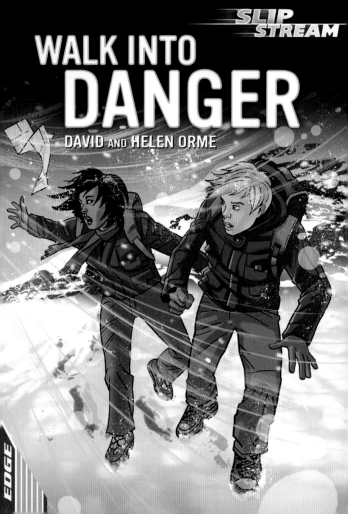

EDGE